Never ask a Dinosaur to Dinner

Written by Gareth Edwards

Illustrated by Guy Parker-Rees

ALISON GREEN BOOKS

Never ask a dinosaur to dinner.
Really, never ask a dinosaur to dinner.

Because a T-Rex is ferocious
And his manners are atrocious,
And you'll find that if he's able . . .

He will eat
the kitchen table!

He'll grow fatter while the rest of you grow thinner,

So **never** ask a dinosaur to dinner.

Please don't share your toothbrush with a shark.
Really, please don't share your
toothbrush with a shark.

They've got so many rows of teeth
On the top and underneath,
And any self-respecting shark'll
Want each little tooth to sparkle.

If you rush him . . .

... he may make a rude remark,

So **please** don't share your toothbrush with a shark.

Never let a beaver in the basin.

Really, never let a beaver
in the basin.

He'll block it up
with sticks and mud,

And turn the taps
on till they flood,

And build a great big beaver dam and
Fill the whole thing up with salmon!

And it won't be very nice
to wash your face in,

So **never** let a beaver in the basin.

Please don't use a tiger as a towel.

Really, **please** don't use
a tiger as a towel.

Because in case you have forgotten
Tigers are not made of cotton,
And although they're furred quite thickly
They can get cross very quickly.

And you'll find they have
a rather scary growl,

So **please** don't use a tiger as a towel.

Never choose a bison for a blanket.

Really, **never** choose a bison for a blanket.

Because although it's warm and woolly
You will find it is a bully,

And its hooves
    will be too clumpy

And its horns
    will make you grumpy,

And by morning-time
you will not want to thank it.

So **never** choose a bison for a blanket.

Please don't let
a barn owl in your bed.
Really, **please** don't let
a barn owl in your bed.

Because the first thing that you'll learn'll
Be a barn owl is nocturnal.
She will hunt for voles and hoot all night
And leave your bed a dreadful sight!

You'll wish that owl
was in a barn instead,

So **please** don't let a barn owl in your bed.

Now, here's how you can have a lovely sleep.
Really, here's how you can have a lovely sleep . . .

Say NO to beaver, shark and owl!
Avoid the tiger and his growl!
Steer clear of every dinosaur!
Leave bison at the bedroom door!

These animals won't help you rest!

At bedtime here is what is best . . .

Stick to ONE teddy . . .

. . . and a flock of sheep.

And THAT'S how you can have a lovely sleep.

For my parents,
with love and
admiration – G.E.

For Peter's
nephew and niece,
Allegra and Monty –
G.P.R.

First published in the UK in 2014 by
Alison Green Books
An imprint of Scholastic Children's Books
Euston House, 24 Eversholt Street
London NW1 1DB
A division of Scholastic Ltd
www.scholastic.co.uk
London – New York – Toronto – Sydney – Auckland
Mexico City – New Delhi – Hong Kong

Text copyright © 2014 Gareth Edwards
Illustrations copyright © 2014 Guy Parker-Rees

HB ISBN: 978 1 407136 92 9
PB ISBN: 978 1 407136 93 6

9 8 7 6 5 4 3 2 1